THE
THREE LITTLE
PIRATES

I'm Tammy

GEORGIE ADAMS
AND EMILY BOLAM

Orion
Children's Books

For Tom — a very special pirate!
With love,
G.A.

First published in Great Britain in 2006
by Orion Children's Books
a division of the Orion Publishing Group Ltd
Orion House
5 Upper St Martin's Lane
London WC2H 9EA

1 3 5 7 9 10 8 6 4 2

Designed by Tracey Cunnell

A catalogue record for this book is available from the British Library

ISBN 10 - 1 84255 519 7
ISBN 13 - 9781 84255 519 4

Printed in Spain

CONTENTS

Meet the Pirates!

I'm Squint!

I'm Scoot!

Ahoy there! Let's meet the three little pirates:

This is Trixy and her dog, Mullet.

Here's Tammy and her lazy cat, Kipper.

And this is Trig. She has a parrot called Gulliver.

Shhh! Don't tell anyone. Mullet's scared of mice!

Shiver me timbers! Yo-ho-ho!

Er, only when they SQUEAK!

Not forgetting the two shipmice, Scoot and Squint.

The three little pirates live aboard their ship, the *Lucky Lobster*.

It has:

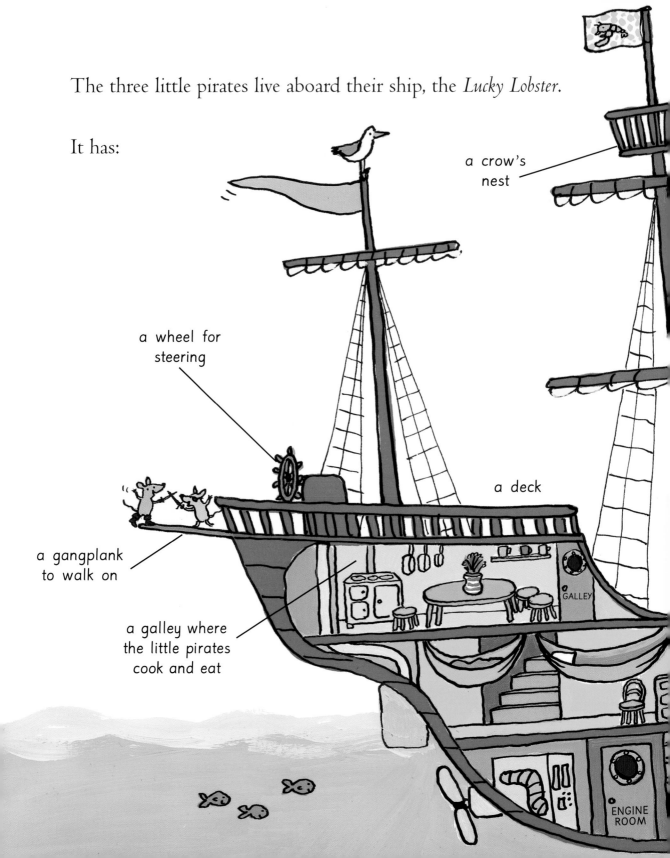

a crow's nest

a wheel for steering

a deck

a gangplank to walk on

a galley where the little pirates cook and eat

GALLEY

ENGINE ROOM

sails for
windy days

hammocks
for
sleeping

portholes to
look through

an engine
for when the
weather is
calm

SUPPLIES

The three little pirates spend their days looking for hidden treasure,

keeping the *Lucky Lobster* ship-shape,

and going to Miss Peggy Leggy's Pirate School for Good
(and sometimes not-so-good!) Little Pirates.

She teaches her pupils
to fire a cannon . . .

Just missed!

Fire!

BOOM!

I hate
this lesson.

Call
the Fire
Brigade!

read treasure maps . . .

and sing rowdy sea songs!

Yo-ho-ho, we're pirates - fearless, bold and brave . . .

And sometimes the little pirates just like playing with their special pirate friends, Toofy and Smudge.

So, now you've met everyone . . .

LET'S GET ON WITH THE STORY!

A Monster, a Mermaid and a Message

One morning Trixy, Tammy and Trig were asleep in their hammocks when . . .

BOOM! BOOM! WHOOOSH!

. . . an enormous wave crashed into the *Lucky Lobster*.

The little pirates woke with a start.

"Limping lugworms!" said Trixy.

Tammy's hammock swung violently. "Jumping jellyfish!" she said.

Trig was under her duvet. She had fallen on the floor!

Crunching crackers! What's happening?

Bilge and barnacles! Ha, ha!

What was that?

It's toooo early.

HELP!

All paws on deck!

It's a rat raid!

Trixy, Tammy and Trig had just enough time to get dressed before . . .

BOOM! WHOOOSH!

A second wave struck the *Lucky Lobster*. The little pirates raced up on deck to see what was going on. And then they heard something that sounded very like a BURP, which was followed by a loud . . .

HICCUP.

Trixy peered over the right side of the boat.

The hiccup was quickly followed by a **boom!** and a **whooosh!** as another wave crashed into them. Tammy got soaked.

"*Glug!* Nothing on the left side," she spluttered.

Suddenly Trig pointed straight ahead. "THERE!" she yelled.

SCREEEEEEEECH!

Abandon ship!

I can't swim.

The little pirates looked and found themselves staring at their friend, Errol the sea monster.

"Sorry about the hiccups. Too much fizzy seaweed pop!" boomed Errol. "I've got an important message for you."

He was about to give them the message when another hiccup rumbled up from his tummy.

hic!

hic!

Here we go again!

Take cover!

Suddenly Tammy remembered a way to stop hiccups. "Hold your breath and count to ten," she said.

Errol looked worried. "I don't know how to count," he said.

"Hold your breath and leave the counting to us," said Trig.

So Errol took a deep breath IN and the little pirates slowly counted to ten.

One . . .

two . . .

three . . .

z-z-z-z-z-z-z!

20

Errol's cheeks puffed up
like pink balloons.

Four . . . five . . .

His eyes rolled.

Six . . . seven . . .

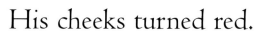

His cheeks turned red.

Eight . . . nine . . .

Bright red.

TEN!

21

Then Errol, bursting for air, breathed out . . .

I'm flying!

PHEWOOOOOOOOOO!

. . . and blew everyone off their feet!

I'm stuck!

Hic, hic, hooray!

22

Trixy waited a moment. "Listen!" she said. There was silence. Errol's hiccups had stopped.

"What about the message?" asked the little pirates.

"Oh, yes," said Errol. "I nearly forgot!"

Errol opened a pouch in his tummy and took out a shiny white pebble. It shone as bright as the moon.

The little pirates peered at the pebble. At first, all they could see was an eerie glow and swirling clouds of mist. Then came a loud ringing tone.

Peep-Peep-dooodley-pip-pip-pip!

The mist cleared and there,
staring out at them, was . . .

a MERMAID!

"My name is Mo," said the mermaid in a faraway voice.
"I'm in trouble. I need your help."

"How can we help you?" asked Trixy.

"Listen!" Mo spoke urgently. "There's a pirate called Vanilla
Cringe . . ."

The little pirates gasped. They all knew about the dreaded
Vanilla Cringe! The sound of her name made them shiver and
go all goose-pimply. Vanilla was the one they feared most — the
meanest, greediest pirate-lady who had ever sailed the Salty Seas.

Trixy, Tammy and Trig had seen some of the villainous things she had done.

Mo went on. "Vanilla's caught my mermates, the slimy toad! She's sold them to a horrid collector. He's locked them up in a glass palace and they'll be there for ever!" she wailed. "Please, please find Vanilla and . . . do something!" said Mo desperately. "She's out to get me too!"

Just then, the glow of the moonstone dimmed, and Mo's image began to fade. "Keep the moonstone safe!" she said. Then she was gone.

Trixy took charge of the moonstone. She put it in her pocket. Meanwhile, Errol (who *might* have been useful) had swum off to buy more seaweed pop.

The little pirates stared at one another. They had to help Mo and her friends somehow. It was the most important thing they had ever been asked to do.

Let's go to Dolphin Island and ask for help. Hurry. There's no time to lose!

But where do we start looking? Mo could be anywhere.

We've got to rescue Mo before that prawn-faced pirate gets her.

Vanilla is a seaslug!

and blobby eyes

With a fat slug body

VANILLA CRINGE

Dribbling slimy stuff

Mo and the Magic Moonstone

Hi! I'm Mo. Just thought you'd like to know a bit more about me and how I came to ask the three little pirates for their help!

Mo lived in the Coral Palace with her father, King Codswallop, and her mother, Queen Pearl. Mo was their only daughter. The king and queen had given the mermaid princess everything she could want. Well, almost. Life at the palace was a bit dull. Not much fun for an adventurous mermaid like Mo!

29

Whenever she could, Mo would sneak past the soldier-crab guards to play around Dolphin Island with her friends. Together they went swimming, dived with the dolphins and explored new and exciting caves.

And Mo might have gone on having fun like this if it hadn't been for that wicked pirate, Vanilla Cringe. Vanilla had been keeping an eye — she had only one — on Mo and her fishy friends for some time. She just had to wait for the right moment.

Then one night,
Vanilla was sailing near
Mermaids' Rock when she saw
Mo and all her friends, playing in the
moonlight. Vanilla punched the air.
Yesssss! It was what she had been waiting
for. She could catch the whole lot in
one go. Vanilla hissed orders to her
crew of sea dogs: Gripe,
Muzzle and Boots.

I'm going to capture the
lot and sell them to the
mermaid collector.
GET FISHING!

There followed a terrible noise and commotion.

"HELP! H-H-H-HELP!" cried the terrified mermaids
and merboys, struggling in the nets.

Mo watched helplessly as her friends, tails thrashing, were slung
aboard the *Slinky Shark*. It made her tail-tingling mad to hear Vanilla
laugh as she threw them into a cage and locked the door.

Triumphantly, Vanilla praised the crew. "Well done, my beauties!" Then, suspiciously, she added, "I trust you got them ALL?"

We may p-p-possibly, have m-m-missed one.

J-j-just the one.

There she is!

"Don't just stand there, nitbrain," yelled Vanilla. "CATCH HER!"

So Gripe frantically fished around with his net. But he couldn't catch Mo. She darted away and hid in a clump of seaweed, her heart thumping. Then Mo overheard Vanilla say crossly: "You've let the prize one get away. She's the princess mermaid. She's worth a fortune! We must catch her later. Come on. Let's take the others to sell to the collector."

Mo had no idea what she meant. Collector? Money? What was that about? And what now? Rush home and tell Mum and Dad? No way! King Codswallop and Queen Pearl would worry their tails off about her. They'd put extra guards on the palace door. Then she'd never get a chance to slip out. What *could* she do?

She was still wondering when her best friend, Errol the sea monster, came along. Errol listened as Mo told him the whole story. Then she said, "What's going on, Errol?"

Errol hadn't a clue, but he could see the *Slinky Shark* heading out to sea.

Hold tight! I can swim faster than you. We'll see where they go.

So they followed Vanilla's ship. Swiftly and silently, Errol swam in its wake until, at last, the *Slinky Shark* dropped anchor. They watched as the cage holding its fishy load was lowered over the side . . .

HELP!

HELP!

Mo dived after it. The water was inky black but she could see easily in the dark. After all, she was a mermaid. What Mo saw next made her gasp . . .

Deep down in the murky depths, was an enormous glass palace. The doors and windows were barred with whalebones, and two fierce-looking swordfish patrolled round and round.

Suddenly, a giant octopus appeared! Mo looked on in horror as the octopus, all eight arms working at once, unlocked the cage and pushed her mermates through the door.

Vanilla has done well. But, let me see, there's one more. Ah, yessss! Princess Mo. The most valuable one of all!

Mo felt a tingling shiver run down her tail. So *this* was the collector she had heard Vanilla talking about. *And I'm next on his list!*

Just then, Errol swam down beside her and Mo quickly told him all she had seen and heard. "Oooo! I'd know that scary monster anywhere," Errol whispered. "It's Hong Kong. He collects . . . things," he added vaguely.

Next they watched Hong Kong struggling to the surface, carrying a heavy bag on each arm.

"And there's more . . . much more . . . when you bring me the princess," wheedled Hong Kong. "She'll be the jewel in my collection. I *must* have her!"

"Got it," whispered Mo angrily. "Vanilla gets paid lots of *money* for her rotten work."

"R-i-g-h-t," said Errol slowly, "and she's out to get you too, remember. So I think we should . . . GO!"

So the two hurried away. Mo's head was spinning. They must try to rescue everyone from that horrid place. But how?

"I know three little pirates who might help," said Errol.

"Really!" said Mo. "Could you give them a message?"

Errol nodded, but Mo wasn't sure. Her friend was very forgetful. By the time Errol had found the little pirates, he would have forgotten what to say! Mo would have gone with him but she had to get home. The night was nearly over and Mo knew she'd be in trouble if she wasn't home before dawn.

Suddenly, Mo remembered a magic moonstone she had been given by a beautiful witch called Sophie. The moonstone looked just like an ordinary pebble but it had magical powers.

burp! hic! hic! phewoooo!

"Phew!" said Mo, quickly taking it out. "I hope I can remember how it works."

Mo closed her eyes and concentrated. She thought really, really hard. Could she get a message to the little pirates through the moonstone?

Meanwhile, Errol had stopped swimming. He was busy slurping a bottle of seaweed pop he had found at the bottom of his pouch. He burped noisily and hiccupped. Mo handed him the moonstone and explained how it worked.

"A message in a pebble? Cool!" said Errol between burps.

Please, give this to the little pirates. When the moonstone rings they'll see me talking to them. It's magic!

So Errol popped the pebble in his pouch and set off to look for the little pirates. It took a while but, at last, early that morning he found the *Lucky Lobster*. To his surprise, when he gave the little pirates the moonstone, it worked. Mo appeared – like magic!

That morning, as Mo made her way home . . . *she was caught!* Vanilla screeched with delight as the crew scooped Mo out of the sea.

"Put me back, Frog Face!" yelled Mo, clawing at the net.

But it was no good. Vanilla picked Mo up by the tail and tossed her into the cage.

"It's off to the collector for you!" cried Vanilla. "I'll get a fortune for you, my princess!"

And so, locked in the cage, Mo screwed her eyes up tight, willing the moonstone to work again. Could she get another message through? Oh, *please*, little pirates, she thought, thinking as hard as she could.

I NEED YOUR HELP RIGHT NOW!

A Surprise Meeting with Vanilla

Back aboard the *Lucky Lobster*, the little pirates sprang into action.

Trig started up the engine and pushed the lever to FAST!

Trixy took the wheel and steered towards Dolphin Island. And Tammy quickly climbed the rigging to the crow's nest. But when she looked through her telescope, she saw a sleek ship, with billowing sails, heading their way.

"Ship straight ahead!" cried Tammy.

As the ship got closer, the little pirates could see a fierce-looking shark on the bow. Tammy recognised the ship at once.

"It's the *Slinky Shark*," she said. "It belongs to Vanilla!"

Suddenly, the awesome figure of Vanilla Cringe came strolling along the deck. She was dressed in a magnificent coat and breeches. Her wild red hair flared like flames. From one ear swung an

enormous gold earring. She looked a terrifying sight. Trixy, Tammy and Trig watched as Vanilla kicked a mouldy cabbage along the deck. Her slobbering pet warthog, Plankton, trotted after the rotten vegetable.

Fetch, Plankton!

Apart from Plankton, the *Slinky Shark* had a motley crew of three sea dogs. (Please read the log for details. Not the log you get from a *tree*! It's a sort of notebook.)

THE LOG OF THE SLINKY SHARK

CAPTAIN
Vanilla Cringe

CREW — 3 Sea Dogs
Gripe

A miserable mongrel who is always complaining!

Muzzle

A bright young pup who was kidnapped by Vanilla Cringe one night when he was asleep in his basket. Has a keen nose for adventure!

Boots

General dogsbody, which means he gets all the rotten jobs, like peeling potatoes and washing up!

44

The *Slinky Shark* was bearing down on them fast. Just in time Trixy spun the wheel and managed to avoid a collision. The *Slinky Shark* went by with a WHOOOOSH! Foaming waves rocked the *Lucky Lobster* from side to side. Vanilla yelled across at them.

Plankton and the sea dogs fell about laughing at Vanilla's feeble joke. They weren't silly. They knew she would have hung them up by their tails if they hadn't! But the sea dogs weren't laughing for long. Vanilla suddenly rounded on them.

"Back to work, you mangy mongrels!" she ordered. "Jump to it or I'll mince you for supper!"

Gripe, Muzzle and Boots hurriedly hoisted another sail, to make the ship go faster. Meanwhile, Plankton, idly wandering about flipping the cabbage from one tusk to another, tripped over a rope . . .

TWANG!

the rope SNAPPED . . .

. . . the sail fell down, and it wrapped them up like a parcel.

Vanilla was eye-popping mad. She turned blotchy purple with rage.

You blockheads!
You blundering
blobs of blubber!

Next, with one hand (though careful not to break her pointy fingernails) she grabbed the rope, and swung the bundle round and round.

I feel
sick

I've been
sick

Phewooooh!

So sorry,
most-beautiful-
lady-pirate!

Aboard the *Lucky Lobster* the little pirates were horrified. They felt sorry for the sea dogs. They even felt sorry for Plankton!

But the *Slinky Shark* had sped Vanilla safely out of earshot. Little did they know how soon they were to meet her again!

Dolphin Island

The little pirates were more determined than ever to find Mo and rescue her mermates. They had seen how mean Vanilla could be! As they sped towards Dolphin Island they hoped their friends, Toofy and Smudge, might help.

Soon the *Lucky Lobster* was chugging into the harbour. Trixy steered the ship to the jetty, Tammy let down the anchor and Trig tied up. Then the three little pirates jumped ashore.

"What shall we do first?" said Trig.

"Let's go and see Toofy and Smudge," said Trixy. "We can go to the Harbour Stores for supplies on our way back." So the three little pirates walked along by Sneaky Creek, to the place where Toofy and Smudge lived.

I'll stay and guard the cheese straws.

Great idea! I'll help too.

Soon they saw the pirate boys busy by the river. The boys appeared to be dismantling a shipwreck.

"Hi!" said Toofy, hitting the wreck with a hammer.

"Great to see you!" said Smudge, staggering under a pile of timber.

"What are you doing?" asked Tammy.

"Making something," said Toofy, mysteriously. "That is, we're unmaking something, to make something else."

"I see," said Tammy. But she didn't really.

Smudge could see the little pirates were puzzled, so he explained. "It's my invention," he said proudly. "Secret, of course, but I *suppose* we can tell you."

WHACK!

Ooo! That made me jump.

"Go on," said Trixy. She hoped it wouldn't take long.

"We're making a . . . submarine!" he said dramatically. "It's for hunting sunken treasure! Brilliant, eh? We'll be the first underwater pirates ever!"

"Yeah," said Toofy. "It'll be really COOL!"

"Aha!" said Trixy, suddenly becoming much more interested in Smudge's invention. "Now a submarine could come in handy . . ." Quickly, she told Toofy and Smudge all about Mo and her mermates.

"We'll help you get 'em!" said Toofy when she had finished.

"You bet!" said Smudge. "Our sub will be just the thing for a mermaid rescue operation!"

Trixy, Tammy and Trig looked in dismay at the mass of broken timbers, twisted metal, hammers, nails and pots of paint that were strewn around the riverbank.

"Er, when will it be ready?" Trig enquired.

"Can't say exactly," said Smudge. "Submarines can be tricky."

"Maybe we could help?" suggested Tammy tactfully. "You know, hurry things along a bit?"

"Hm! Don't know about that," said Toofy, striking the wreck with an ear-splitting CRASH. "It's a delicate business . . ."

"Oh, come off it!" said Smudge. "We could do with a hand. Six, actually! You know, three little pirates . . . six hands . . ."

Toofy grinned. "Yeah, yeah! I can count!" he said.

So, Trixy, Tammy and Trig spent a while helping Toofy and Smudge make their submarine. They had great fun sawing, hammering, fetching, carrying and sloshing paint over everything! The submarine was taking shape FAST.

The little pirates could see that the submarine was nearly ready, so they told Toofy and Smudge it was time for them to go.

"Thanks for your help," said the boys.

"See you later!" shouted Trixy, Tammy and Trig.

Then they hurried off to the Harbour Stores. As they went along, the little pirates made a note of the things they needed to buy.

"We'll need food, a map and stuff like that," said Trixy.

"And sweets!" said Trig. "Skulls and Bones. Yummy!"

Meanwhile, Tammy was thinking. "We need to know more about mermaids, and where to look for them," she said.

"Don't forget we have the moonstone!" said Trixy, patting her pocket. "With any luck, Mo will tell us where she is."

"But if something happens to Mo . . ." began Tammy.

Trixy knew what she meant. "You're right," she said.

"Mr Spoons might have a book about mermaids," said Tammy hopefully, as they reached the Harbour Stores.

And Jolly Polly parrot seed!

Mr Spoons was very pleased to see them. "Can I help you?" he said.

"What are you looking for today?"

"A torch, a map of Dolphin Island, three swimming costumes, Skulls and Bones, seaweed pop . . ."

Can YOU find all the things on the pirates' shopping list?

RELAX! We sell hammocks

FORK HANDLES

PRAWN FLAKES

PRAWN FLAKES

CLAM & VINEGAR CRISPS

SKULLS & BONES

A Pirate's Life

The Three Little Pirates

Pirate Spotting

All About Pirates

A Brief History of MERMAIDS

Mermaids

Teach your Parrot to Talk

SPOTTED HEAD SCARVES

JOLLY POLLY parrot seed

A large packet
of prawnflakes,
a notebook and pencil,
Meaty Matey, Purrkins,
Jolly Polly seed . . .

. . . and mermaids,
anything you've got
on mermaids.

PURRKINS

CUTLASS

FOR EXPERIENCED PIRATES ONLY!

"Aah," said Mr Spoons. "Mermaids! Fascinating creatures! I believe they're an endangered species?"

"Yes," said Tammy. "We happen to know some who are." And she told Mr Spoons all they knew about Mo.

Mr Spoons looked worried and said: "Mo is the only daughter of King Codswallop and Queen Pearl! If anything were to happen . . ."

Dead-eyed dogfish! There WAS something about a mermaid in the Dolphin Times. It's around here . . . somewhere.

DOLPHIN ISLAND M

TREASURE MAP

SWIMMING RESULTS

IT'S A GAME OF TWO HALVES

THE DOLPHIN TIMES

A FISHY BUSINESS

LATE NEWS EXTRA

A coastguard reported seeing a mermaid in distress around the Quicksand Bay area. Pirates with large fishing nets were seen acting suspiciously.

The little pirates crowded round and read the newspaper together.

"Fishhooks!" exclaimed Trixy. "That could be Mo!" The others groaned. "And those suspicious pirates . . ."

"Vanilla and her crew!" said Mr Spoons. "Do you think they've caught Mo already!"

"I've a horrible feeling you're right," said Trig. "Do you know anyone who could help us find her?"

"Hm!" said Mr Spoons. "Give me a tick-tock. You do your shopping and I'll have a think."

So Trixy and Trig quickly hunted round for the things they wanted to buy.

Meanwhile Tammy went to look at some books. She found two about mermaids.

This is what she read:

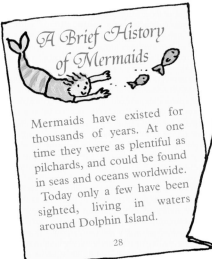

A Brief History of Mermaids

Mermaids have existed for thousands of years. At one time they were as plentiful as pilchards, and could be found in seas and oceans worldwide.
Today only a few have been sighted, living in waters around Dolphin Island.

28

All About Mermaids
a beginner's guide

Chapter 1
Know Your Mermaids

Mermaids prefer to swim underwater during the day and surface at night. The best time for spotting mermaids is during a full moon, when they may be seen moonbathing on rocks. There are a number of species. The main difference is in the tail.

4

Know Your Mermaids

The chart below shows five types of common mermaid.

The Flick Tail
The Swish Tail
The Long Tail
The Short Tail
The Fan Tail

5

When they were ready, the three little pirates went to the checkout. Mr Spoons was waiting for them with a smile on his face. He had thought of someone who might help.

"Go and see Sophie. She lives at Quicksand Bay," he said. "She knows Mo and the king and queen. Sophie can't speak but she has . . . *special powers.*"

"Great!" said the little pirates. "Thank you."

They paid for their shopping, which came to twelve golden gillies and six silver scuttles, then walked back to the *Lucky Lobster*.

And at that very moment, the moonstone in Trixy's pocket went . . .

Peep-peep-dooodley-pip-pip-pip!

Sophie, Clues and a Puzzle

Trixy, Tammy and Trig stared at the moonstone. As before, there were clouds of mist but this time the mist did not clear. They could just make out the hazy figure of Mo. She appeared to be in a cage.

"Oh, no!" wailed Trixy. "Mo's been caught."

"Where are you?" cried Tammy.

Her voice was the tiniest whisper.

"Ssssh!" said Trig.

"She must be in that collector's place," said Tammy.

"And where's that?" said Trig.

Before the little pirates could ask Mo, the moonstone faded. Once again, it looked like an ordinary pebble.

"We must go and see Sophie," said Trixy. "Mr Spoons said she might help."

The little pirates looked at the map of Dolphin Island – the one Trixy had bought earlier. They soon found Quicksand Bay where Sophie lived.

"We can cross Sneaky Creek by the rope bridge," said Tammy, "and follow the footpaths from there."

So the little pirates set off. They took seaweed pop and crisps to eat on the way. Trig remembered to take her new notebook and pencil.

Near the rope bridge they saw Toofy and Smudge, putting the finishing touches to the submarine.

The three little pirates put their thumbs up. "Good luck!" they cried and hurried over the bridge.

There were two footpaths — one straight ahead and the other to the right. Trixy went to look at the map to see which footpath they should take. "Oh no!" she groaned. "I've forgotten the map."

"Let's flip a coin and decide that way," said Tammy brightly. She took a silver scuttle from her pocket which had a fish on one side and a crab on the other.

"Fish side up, we go right. Crab, straight ahead," she said, tossing the scuttle in the air.

It landed crab side up. "Straight on!" said Trixy.

It turned out to be quite a long walk, which took them past the
Coastguard's Cottage and along the cliffs to Quicksand Bay. The
little pirates clambered down a steep, rocky path to the beach. The
tide was out, so they ran along the sand, looking around for Sophie.

Trixy scrambled up a sand dune. She pointed to a little wooden
hut. It was painted the brightest blue and decorated with
pebbles and shells.

BEWARE
QUICKSAND

Look!

I wish we'd
brought our new
swimsuits.

No time for
swimming!

"It must be Sophie's hut," said Tammy. Her words faded away when, out of nowhere, a beautiful girl appeared. She had long golden hair and wore a necklace of seashells. It was Sophie.

Sophie greeted them, smiling. She knew exactly why the little pirates had come. That very morning she had seen Vanilla and her crew fish Mo out of the sea, at Quicksand Bay.

Sophie beckoned the little pirates to follow, taking them to a rock pool by the sea. It was a magic pool and only Sophie could see people and places in it. She knelt down and gazed into the water.

After a while, Sophie stood up and drew some pictures in the sand.

Sophie nodded eagerly. Then, suddenly, Trig gave a shout. "Look! The tide is coming in. The sea will wash them away!"

"Flipping flatfish!" cried Trixy. "Quick, Trig! Copy them in your notebook. We'll work them out later."

So Trig copied Sophie's picture clues, like this.

Now the little pirates couldn't wait to get back to the *Lucky Lobster* to work out Sophie's clues. But which way should they go?

"We can't go back along the beach," said Trixy anxiously.

Tammy looked at Sophie. "Is there another way?" she asked.

Sophie pointed to a quicker way. Before the little pirates left, she gave them each a necklace of seashells.

This necklace is just like yours!

Thank you!

I'm sure they're special. They'll help us.

Then the little pirates hurried back to their ship.

After they had gone, Sophie took a reed-pipe and played a tune. All at once, three friendly dolphins leaped out of the sea. They listened to Sophie's music – it was her way of talking to them.

When she stopped playing, they swam off to deliver a very important message to King Codswallop and Queen Pearl.

On board the *Lucky Lobster* the little pirates looked at the picture clues in Trig's notebook.

"A key," said Trixy, pointing to the first clue. "To a door . . ."

"A door . . . in a cage!" said Tammy. "Mo's in a cage. We saw her in the moonstone, remember?"

"Right," said Trig, now looking at the second clue. "And the shark's easy. That *has* to be the *Slinky Shark*, I reckon. Vanilla's got Mo in a cage, on board the *Slinky Shark*."

"Good," said Trixy. "Now we're getting somewhere."

"Not really," said Tammy. "We know Vanilla's got Mo. But *where* is she going?"

"Well, what about the octopus?" said Trixy.

The three little pirates looked puzzled.

"Maybe he's . . . the collector?" suggested Tammy.

"Could be," said Trixy. "But he could be *anywhere*."

They all looked at the last clue.

"A man's head . . ." said Tammy slowly.

"A bald head," said Trig. "What does *that* mean?"

Suddenly Trixy grabbed the map of Dolphin Island. "Look!" she said. "*Bald Head*. It's on the map. Vanilla is making for Bald Head."

The little pirates cheered. They sang and pranced round the deck.

YO-HO-HO!

Let's GO-GO-GO

and CATCH HER!

A Race Against Time!

The little pirates were very excited. They had worked out Sophie's clues and discovered that Mo was aboard the *Slinky Shark,* and it was sailing towards Bald Head.

"It's halfway round the island," said Trixy. "We'll have to move fast, to catch her!"

There was no time to lose. Tammy scrambled up to the crow's nest. She would be keeping a sharp lookout for Vanilla's ship, through her telescope. To her dismay, she saw black clouds out at sea. Then they all heard a rumble of thunder.

Ooo! I'm scared.

Looks like we're in for a storm!

Yo-ho-ho!

"Hoist the mainsail!" cried Trixy. "Let's go!"

"Wait!" said Trig. "We've forgotten to tell Toofy and Smudge where we're going."

Trig was about to jump ashore when the pirate boys came along in their submarine.

Close behind was Errol, the sea monster. He had been drinking seaweed pop at the Harbour Stores, and was curious to see this new monster. Errol *burped* and caused a minor tidal wave.

The submarine bobbed up and down with Toofy at the controls.

"Follow us!" shouted Trig. "You, too, Errol!"

And so the little pirates, Toofy, Smudge and Errol set off to rescue Mo. It was early evening. The storm was gathering force, and the *Lucky Lobster*'s sails filled with wind. Soon they were out of the harbour and battling through heavy seas. It was pouring with rain too.

Suddenly Tammy gave a shout: "*Slinky Shark* ahead!"

Trixy, at the wheel, peered through the rain. It was Vanilla's ship, sure enough. The chase was on!

Ship ahoy!

Aboard the *Slinky Shark*, Vanilla was screaming orders at the sea dogs. Gripe, Muzzle and Boots struggled to haul up another sail. The ship pitched and rolled. Thunder boomed overhead. Whilst the crew worked their paws off, Vanilla's pet warthog, Plankton, leaned over the side. His stomach was churning like a food-mixer, and he had turned an alarming shade of green.

And nearby, tossed around in a cage, was Mo! She clung to the bars as the cage slid wildly from one side of the deck to the other.

Meanwhile, the *Lucky Lobster* was steadily catching up. The storm had slowed the *Slinky Shark* and before long, the little pirates were not far behind. Then Trig spotted Mo.

"There she is!" she cried.

At that moment, Errol, who had been rolling about in the waves, gave an enormous . . . HICCUP! The seaweed pop in his tummy erupted like a volcano. It was his biggest hiccup ever!

A wave as big as a mountain crashed into the *Slinky Shark*. It sent Mo's cage skidding across the deck . . . over the side and INTO THE SEA.

BOOM! WHOOOSH!

SPLASH!

Vanilla couldn't believe her eyes. Her prize mermaid had just gone overboard. She was furious. "Get her back!" she yelled.

Unfortunately for Vanilla, neither Gripe, Muzzle nor Boots could swim. As for Plankton . . . well, he was being sick!

The little pirates gasped as the cage fell into the sea. "We must get her out!" said Tammy, scrambling down the rigging.

"You go with Trig!" said Trixy. "I'll steer the ship."

So Tammy and Trig put on their swimsuits and dived overboard. They were still wearing Sophie's necklaces. They kicked their legs and swam deeper and deeper. The little pirates found they could swim better than ever. And, most surprisingly, they could BREATHE underwater too.

We can swim like fish with these necklaces!

And Errol, swimming happily alongside, turned a somersault. Next, a huge creature with bright yellow eyes, came gliding towards them. At first Tammy and Trig thought it was a shark. But it was only Toofy and Smudge in their submarine. What the pirates had mistaken for eyes were two powerful headlights. The beams shone through the murky water, and picked out something on the seabed.

Look! It's Mo's cage.

HELP!

In a flash, Tammy and Trig zoomed down and opened the door.
"Thanks!" said Mo. "I knew you'd come."
"Errol helped too!" they said.

When the little pirates and Mo were safely back on board, Trixy pointed to the *Slinky Shark*. It was *behind* them. While the others had been rescuing Mo, Trixy had managed to take the lead. Now Vanilla was chasing them!

That meddling mollusc won't stop till she catches me.

Not if we can help it.

"We've got to rescue your friends. You know the way, right?" said Trixy.

Mo nodded. So while Trixy steered a course for Bald Head, Tammy and Trig worked the sails. The wind blew its hardest. It tossed the *Lucky Lobster* about like a cork, and the *Slinky Shark* was gathering speed. Would the little pirates get to the collector's place before Vanilla caught up with them?

smash, Grab and a Battle!

Vanilla Cringe paced the deck of the *Slinky Shark*, scowling. She could see the *Lucky Lobster* ahead. It was right over Hong Kong's palace. Vanilla saw Mo guiding the little pirates to the very spot!

"I'll get that mermaid back somehow!" she muttered.

When the two boats were close enough, Vanilla saw her chance. She grabbed a rope, made a lasso and let it fly. *Swish!*

Aboard the *Lucky Lobster*, Trixy saw it coming. "Look out, Mo!" she warned.

Mo tried to escape by diving overboard. Too late! Vanilla had caught her in midair. "GOTCHA!" she cried gleefully.

The little pirates groaned. But there was nothing they could do for Mo just then.

"Don't worry about me," said Mo. "Rescue the others first."

So Trixy, Tammy and Trig jumped into the sea together.

Down, down, down. The little pirates swam, as fast as fishes, to the bottom of the sea. And there, straight ahead, was the palace!

The little pirates gasped. It was huge!

Tammy pointed to Mo's friends, who were trapped behind a thick glass wall.

Lumping limpets!

Look!

There must be a way in.

They were busy looking at the wall when *SWOOOSH!* two fierce swordfish swam round a corner.

"Guards!" wailed Trig. "Now we're for it!"

The guards headed straight for the little pirates, but before they could attack, Toofy and Smudge zoomed by. The submarine took the swordfish by surprise. This thing looked dangerous!

Aim for the door!

Right!

There was an earsplitting CRASH! as the submarine smashed through the bars, and seconds later, everyone swam out.

WOWEEE!

We're free!

"We're sunk!" moaned Toofy and Smudge . . . which was true. The submarine was badly damaged and they couldn't swim. One little merboy rushed to help. He had just reached the submarine when a sticky tentacle grabbed him round the middle. The collector was out of his lair!

Hong Kong lunged at the escaping mermaids and merboys.
Eight squirming tentacles whirred around like windmills. But as
fast as he could squeeze them, the little pirates struggled to set
them free. It was like unwrapping parcels tied with wriggly string.

It was a tremendous battle: three little pirates against one gigantic
monster. But one by one, Mo's friends swam to safety. Then Trixy,
Tammy and Trig helped the pirate boys out of their submarine.

HELP! It's
Hong Kong!

Meanwhile, Vanilla had been waiting for Hong Kong to appear. She usually lowered her victims down to him in a cage. But the cage, you'll remember, had been lost. This time, Hong Kong would have to come and collect the mermaid himself.

Vanilla dangled Mo over the side, like bait . . .

Suddenly, a thrashing tentacle broke the surface. Hong Kong was frothing with rage. His palace had been smashed to bits, his mermaid collection gone. Now he lashed out at anything going. One l-o-n-g tentacle flicked across the deck and coiled round Vanilla's boots.

"AAAAAARH!" she screamed.

Ugh!
D-I-S-G-U-S-T-I-N-G

Plankton and the crew were just in time to see her disappear beneath the waves.

Mo giggled helplessly. "Wicked!" she cried. With a flick of her tail, she swam back to the *Lucky Lobster*.

Hong Kong dragged his victim down. He didn't know it was Vanilla. Next he squirted her with stinky black INK!

Hong Kong was horrified when he saw his mistake.

"Ooops! Sorr-e-e-e-e," he said. Vanilla came up gulping for air. "G-E-T M-E O-U-T!" she spluttered.

The sea dogs hauled her aboard. The once terrifying pirate lady had become a bedraggled mess. She was dribbling inky goo.

But there was worse to come.

Remember the message Sophie had sent to King Codswallop? Well, when the king heard what Vanilla Cringe was up to, he ordered his army to pay her a visit . . .

Suddenly, out of the sea, came HUNDREDS of soldier crabs! They marched on to the ship, with their sword-sharp pincers.

"OW! OW! OW!" cried Vanilla. But they would not stop.

By this time, everyone on board the *Lucky Lobster* could see what was happening. There were Trixy, Tammy and Trig and the pirate boys and Mo and all her friends. You should have heard them cheer!

Vanilla knew when she was beaten. She had been pinched all over. And, thanks to the little pirates, she had lost a fortune. "I never want to see you lot again. EVER!" she screamed. After that, Vanilla and her crew took off as fast as they could go. It was the last anyone saw of them.

But Trixy looked worried.

Mo was right. Hong Kong had given up mermaid-collecting. He went back to his lair and was never heard of again.

A Party for the Pirates!

The moon shone bright and clear as the *Lucky Lobster* drifted into the harbour. The storm had passed, the sea was calm and everyone was happy.

Trixy, Tammy and Trig were surprised to find a crowd waiting by the jetty. They were greeted with shouts and cheers.

Well done, little pirates. Hooray!

Cool!

Somehow Mr Spoons had heard all about their battle with Hong Kong and Vanilla's encounter with the crabs. The news had flashed round Dolphin Island like lightning.

"Clumping clams!" exclaimed Trixy.

"Fishcakes!" said Tammy.

"We did a good job!" said Trig.

As everyone was coming ashore, they heard a fanfare of trumpets. *Toot-toot-toodle-do. Tan-tan-terrah!*

The soldier crabs stood smartly to attention.

"It's my mum and dad!" cried Mo.

Sure enough, King Codswallop and Queen Pearl had just arrived. They were sitting in a splendid sea-carriage, drawn by flying-fish.

The king and queen were very pleased to see Mo again. Their tails went *flip, flap, flip!* Next, King Codswallop made a speech. The king thanked the little pirates for bravely rescuing his daughter and all her friends. He congratulated Toofy and Smudge, and gave a special mention to Errol, whose hiccups had been really useful. But when King Codswallop (who just loved talking!) started to ramble on about other things, Mo rolled her eyes and cried, "D-A-D!"

So the king stopped talking, and Queen Pearl presented the awards. First, there were gold medals for Trixy, Tammy and Trig. "For being Very Brave Little Pirates!" said the queen.

There was a box of treasure for Toofy and Smudge. And an extra-large bottle of seaweed pop for Errol. Suddenly there was a terrific BANG! followed by a fizzing Z-Z-Z-Z-OOOOOM! Then a million stars burst into the sky.

It's PARTY TIME!

O-o-o-o!

Z Z Z

Fireworks.
I'm off!

Everyone had a wonderful time.

Yo-ho-ho and a
bottle of GUM!

91

When, at last, it was time for them all to go to bed, three sleepy little pirates climbed into their hammocks.

"Goodnight, Trixy."   "Goodnight, Tammy."   "Goodnight, Trig."

Goodnight, little pirates.

Goodnight!

DOLPHIN ISLAND

N
W E
S

FOOTPATH

HARBOUR
STORES

BARNACLE
BEACH

LIGHTHOUSE

LIBRARY

THE
HARBOUR

JETTY

THE SALTY SEAS